To the McLellan clan—not a party pooper among you!
—GM

To Josie.
—LS

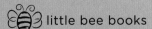 little bee books

251 Park Avenue South, New York, NY 10010
Text copyright © 2020 by Gretchen McLellan
Illustrations copyright © 2020 by Lucy Semple
Library of Congress Cataloging-in-Publication Data
Names: McLellan, Gretchen Brandenburg, author. | Semple, Lucy, illustrator.
Title: No party poopers! / by Gretchen Brandenburg McLellan; illustrated by
Lucy Semple. | Description: First edition. | New York, NY: Little Bee, [2020]
Summary: Two bears decide to throw a party, but the stereotypes one
has about all of their neighbors leave them with no one to invite.
Identifiers: LCCN 2019018004 | Subjects: | CYAC: Parties—Fiction. |
Bears—Fiction. | Animals—Fiction. | Stereotypes (Social psychology)—Fiction.
Classification: LCC PZ7.1.M4627 No 2020 | DDC [E]—dc23
LC record available at https://lccn.loc.gov/2019018004

Manufactured in China   LEO 0420
First Edition   10 9 8 7 6 5 4 3 2 1
ISBN 978-1-4998-0988-6
For more information about special discounts on bulk purchases,
please contact Little Bee Books at sales@littlebeebooks.com.

littlebeebooks.com

NO PARTY POOPERS!

By Gretchen McLellan

Illustrations by Lucy Semple

Hey, let's have a **party**!

Great idea! Who should we invite?

All the Bears, of course.

Why don't we mix it up and invite everybody in our neighborhood!

Everybody? I don't know everybody. I don't want any party poopers to come.

We can invite the Rhinos.
They aren't party poopers.

But the Rhinos would
pop the balloons.

I love balloons.

Okay . . . then how about the Giraffes?

They'd tangle the streamers!

Well, what about the Monkeys?

They'd swing from the piñatas and break them.

Then let's invite the Goats.
They can't climb that high.

Yeah, but they'd chew up the party hats.
Plus, they'd butt into everybody's business.

How do you know?

The Elephants said so and
they never forget a thing.

Do you want the Elephants to come?

No way! They'd smash
the bounce house.

Then how about the Sloths?
They won't break anything.

But they'd never show up on time.

Can we invite the Camels?

They'd drain the pool.
Plus, they spit and drool.

The Raccoons
are clean.

Too clean!
They'd steal the cake
and wash it!

The Pigs?

Would make a mess of everything
and hog all the honey buns, too.

The Porcupines are neat.

But they'd kebab the fruit.

The Donkeys?

Won't stick around
for the games.

The Crows?

Hoard all the
shiny prizes.

The Skunks?

Will make a stink
if they don't win.

The Owls are a hoot!

Bunch of wise guys!

The Geese?

Gossips!

And their feathers
make me sneeze.

The Peacocks?

Show-offs!

The Parrots?   Copycats!

The Rabbits?

There are just too
many of them.

The Dogs and Cats?

Catastrophe!

What's happening
over there?

A party.

Can I come, too?

Sorry. No party poopers.

I'm not a party pooper.

Really?

I'm not!
Can I come,
please?

You won't know everyone.

I know, but I'll be brave.

And friendly and fun?

Yes, friendly and fun, too. I promise.
I know what I'll do. I'll try to be like you!
You're not a party pooper!

Thanks!

Then I can come?

Sure. Let's PARTY!

Why didn't you tell me our neighbors are so much fun? They aren't at all like I expected!

Mixing it up is fun, isn't it?

Yeah! Hey, I've got a great idea.
Let's invite everybody to *our* party!

It was PAWSitively
the best party ever.

FREE
·○ BEAR ○·
HUGS!